Come Here, Tiger!

Alex Moran

Illustrated by Lisa Campbell Ernst

Green Light Readers
Harcourt, Inc.
San Diego   New York   London

www.harcourt.com

First Green Light Readers edition 2001
Green Light Readers is a trademark of Harcourt, Inc.,
registered in the United States of America and/or other jurisdictions.

Library of Congress Cataloging-in-Publication Data
Moran, Alex.
Come here, Tiger/by Alex Moran; illustrated by Lisa Campbell Ernst.
p.   cm.
"Green Light Readers."
Summary: A little girl encounters various animals before finding her cat.
[1. Cats—Fiction. 2. Lost and found possessions—Fiction.]
I. Ernst, Lisa Campbell, ill. II. Title. III. Green Light reader.
PZ7.M788193Co 2001
[E]—dc21   00-9726
ISBN 0-15-216218-6
ISBN 0-15-216225-9 (pb)

A C E G H F D B
A C E G H F D B (pb)

Come Here, Tiger!

Come here, Tiger.

Where is that cat?

Is that cat in the bed?

No, it's Scotty!

Come here, Tiger.
Is that cat in the box?

No, it's Rabbit!

Come here, Tiger.
Is that cat in the tub?

No, it's Frog!

Come here, Tiger.
Is that cat in the hat?

No, it's Turtle!

Come here, Tiger.
Where are you, Tiger?

Look! Here you are!

Meet the Illustrator

Lisa Campbell Ernst loves to illustrate books about animals. Before she painted the pictures for **Come Here, Tiger,** she thought about her own pets. They became the models for the animals in this story. Lisa Campbell Ernst's daughter became the model for the girl who is looking for Tiger!

Lisa Campbell Ernst